WHERE'S OUR MAMA?

• • •

DIANE GOODE

A PUFFIN UNICORN

for my mama

with grateful acknowledgment
to Lucia Monfried

PUFFIN UNICORN BOOKS

Published by the Penguin Group
Penguin Books USA Inc., 375 Hudson Street, New York, New York 10014, USA
Penguin Books Ltd, 27 Wrights Lane, London W8 5TZ, England
Penguin Books Australia Ltd, Ringwood, Victoria, Australia
Penguin Books Canada Ltd, 10 Alcorn Avenue, Toronto, Ontario, Canada M4V 3B2
Penguin Books (N.Z.) Ltd, 182-190 Wairau Road, Auckland 10, New Zealand
Penguin Books Ltd, Registered Offices: Harmondsworth, Middlesex, England

Copyright © 1991 by Diane Goode
All rights reserved.
Unicorn is a registered trademark of Dutton Children's Books,
a division of Penguin Books USA Inc.
Library of Congress number 91-2158
ISBN 0-14-055555-2
Published in the United States by Dutton Children's Books,
a division of Penguin Books USA Inc.
Designer: Riki Levinson
Printed in Hong Kong by South China Printing Co.
First Puffin Unicorn Edition 1995
1 3 5 7 9 10 8 6 4 2

WHERE'S OUR MAMA? is also available in hardcover from Dutton Children's Books.

When we arrived in the station, a big gust of wind blew mama's hat right off her head. "Oh, la la!" she cried. "Stay right here while I find it."

Mama ran after her hat
while we sat and waited,

and waited.

When mama still did not return, we began
to cry.
A gendarme nearby heard us.
"We have lost our mother," we sobbed.
"What is her name?" he asked.
"Mama."
"What does your mama look like?"
"Our mama is the most beautiful woman
in the world!"
"Dry your eyes, children, and we will
find her."

"Is this your mama?" asked the gendarme.
"Oh, no, sir. Our mama is very strong.
Mama can carry her own parcels."

"Is this your mama?"

"Oh, no, sir. Our mama doesn't read the newspaper. Mama reads books—millions of books."

"Is this your mama?"
"Oh, no, sir. Our mama never whispers.
Everyone loves mama's voice—she is
famous for it."

"Is that your mama?"

"Oh, no, sir. Our mama is very slim. But Mama cooks the best food in the world."

"Is this your mama?"
"Oh, no, sir. Our mama wears only
pretty hats."

"Is that your mama?"

"Oh, no, sir. Our mama is not afraid of
a mouse. Mama is very brave."

"Is that your mama?"

"Oh, no, sir. Our mama would never do that. She is very smart."

"Is that your mama?"
"Oh, no, sir. People listen when our mama speaks. Oh! I just remembered what mama said."

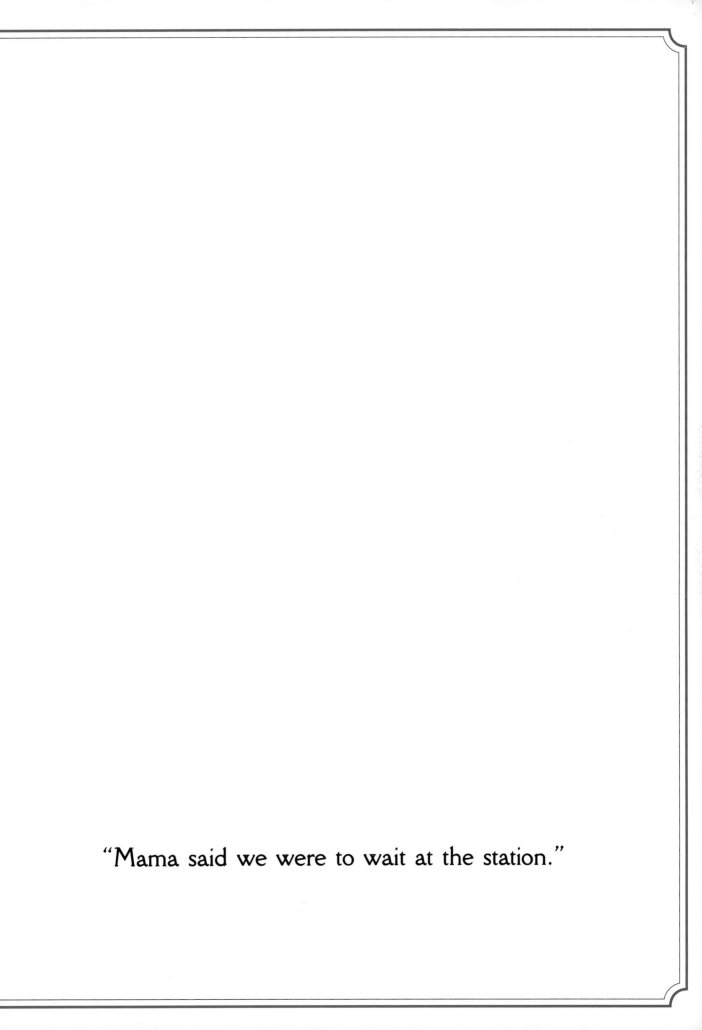

"Mama said we were to wait at the station."

"Is this your mama?"

"Yes, this is our mama!"